2

My Holiday in

Poland

Susie Brooks

WAYLAND

First published in 2008 by Wayland

Copyright © Wayland 2008

Wayland
338 Euston Road
London NW1 3BH

Wayland Australia
Level 17/207 Kent Street
Sydney NSW 2000

Senior Editor: Claire Shanahan
Designer: Elaine Wilkinson
Map artwork: David le Jars

Brooks, Susie
My holiday in Poland
1. Vacations - Poland - Juvenile literature 2. Recreation -
Poland - Juvenile literature 3. Poland - Juvenile
literature 4. Poland - Social life and customs -
Juvenile literature
I. Title II. Poland
914.3'8'0457

ISBN 978 0 7502 5330 7

Cover: skating on a market square, Wroclaw, © Andrzej Gorzkowski/Alamy; traditional dancing at the Krakow
Festival of Children, © Jacek Bednarczyk/PAP/Corbis.

p5: © Frank Chmura/Alamy; p6: © Bartlomiej Zborowski/PAP/Corbis; p7: © Andrzej Gorzkowski/Alamy; p8: ©
Roger Mardon/Alamy; p9: © Raymond Gehman/Corbis; p10: © imagebroker/Alamy; p11: © Rainer Jahns/Alamy; p12:
© Jose Fuste Raga/Corbis; p13: © Dallas and John Heaton/Free Agents Limited/Corbis; p14, title page: © Philippe
Giraud/Goodlook/Corbis; p15: © Interfoto Pressebildagentur/Alamy; p16: © les polders/Alamy; p17: © Dallas and
John Heaton/Free Agents Limited/Corbis; p18: © David Sutherland/Corbis; p19: © Stefan Sauer/dpa/Corbis; p20:
© Paul Gapper/Alamy; p21: © Simon Reddy/Alamy; p22: © James Nazz/Corbis; p23: © Franz-Marc Frei/Corbis;
p24: © Paul Almasy/Corbis; p25: © Christophe Boisvieux/Corbis; p26: © Pegaz/Alamy; p27: © Jacek
Bednarczyk/PAP/Corbis; ©; p28: © Paul Gapper/Alamy; p29: © Robert Clare/Alamy; © Harry Rhodes/Wishlist
Images 2008; p31: © Christophe Boisvieux/Corbis.

Printed in China

Wayland is a division of Hachette Children's Books, an Hachette Livre UK company.

www.hachettelivre.co.uk

Contents

This is Poland!

Poland is a beautiful country in the middle of Europe. You can fly here by aeroplane, or take a train, bus or car through other European countries.

These are some places to visit. Look out for them later in the book.

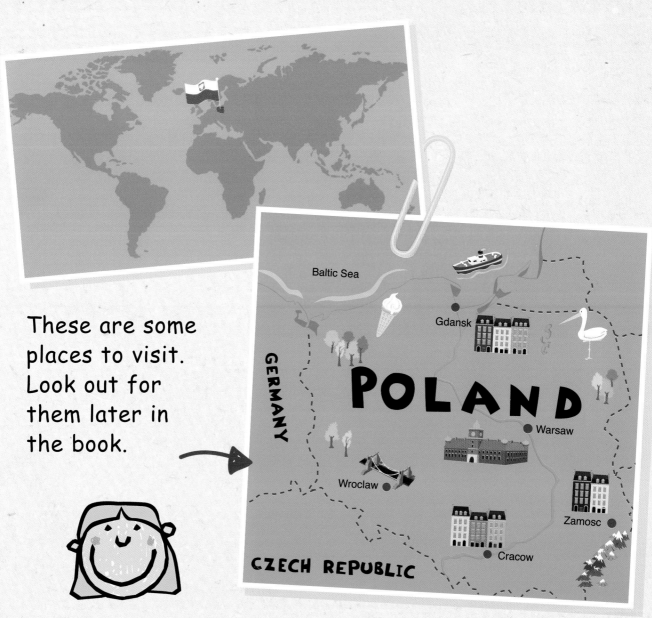

When you get to Poland, some things will seem like home – and others won't. The Polish language sounds very different from English.

Your Polish adventure might start here, in Warsaw airport.

I had to put my watch forward by one hour when I got to Poland!

Speak Polish!

hello/hi
cześć (**chesh**-ch)

please
prosze (**pro**-shuh)

thank you
dziękuje (jen-**koo**-ye)

When to go

It's hard to know what to expect from the weather in Poland – it changes a lot! Spring and summer are hot, but they can be very rainy, too.

In summer, it's usually warm enough for a swim, even on a cloudy day.

Ice skating is a fun way to warm up in winter.

Many people visit Poland in early autumn, when there is sunshine and little rain. Winter can be very cold and snowy, especially in the mountains.

Things to take

- suncream
- shorts and t-shirts
- raincoat

Where to stay

Most visitors to Poland stay in hotels in towns and cities, or near to the sea. Others find rooms in guest houses with Polish families.

In the mountains, many people live in 'gingerbread' houses like this one in Zakopane.

Poland has several **spa towns**, where people go to be cured by healing waters. You can also stay on a farm and learn about life in the countryside.

It's fun to help out on a Polish farm.

 We stayed in a farmhouse with a thatched roof.

I got woken up by a noisy cockerel every morning!

Getting around

A great way to travel in many parts of Poland is by water. You can take a barge along a **canal**, canoe across a lake or even ride a raft down a river.

Parts of the Ostrodzko-Elbląski Canal are dry, so boats have to be dragged along on wheels until they reach the next bit of water!

In some Polish cities people travel by **tram**, while in the countryside horses are still a handy means of transport.

If you ride a horse-drawn sledge in winter, remember to wear warm clothes.

On Polish roads

- People drive on the right-hand side of the road.
- Children under 10 mustn't travel in the front without a safety seat.

Welcome to Warsaw

Many holidays to Poland start in Warsaw, the capital city. It is an exciting mix of old and new streets, houses, palaces and parks.

This is the Palace of Culture and Science. Close to the top, there is a terrace you can visit for a great view of the city.

The cheeky squirrels in Łazienki Park stole some of our picnic!

Visitors can hire boats on the lake beside the palace in Łazienki Park.

In the old part of Warsaw, you can follow the Royal Route from the Royal Castle to Wilanów Palace, where the king used to stay in summer.

Don't miss

A ride - on the electric sightseeing train

A walk - along the Old Town walls or in the dry castle moat

A show - at the Guliwer Children's Theatre

Rainbow towns

These decorative buildings surround Zamość market square.

Wherever you go in Poland, you'll see beautiful buildings. Many of them are painted in bright, cheerful colours.

Gdańsk is an important town because the **Second World War** began here. Bombs turned the town to rubble, but now it has been rebuilt.

There is a wonderful clock inside St Mary's Church in Gdańsk.

Other towny trips

Wroclaw - count the 100 bridges!

Sopot - skip along Europe's longest wooden pier

Częstochowa - visit the famous Jasna Góra monastery

Day adventures

Taking a day trip from the town you are staying in is a good way to explore parts of Poland. Here are a few ideas.

From Warsaw

Visit the Kampinos National Park – in autumn you can join Polish families picking mushrooms in the forest.

From Cracow

Go deep underground in the Wieliczka Salt Mine – you'll find tunnels, lakes and even chapels carved out of the salt!

From Gdańsk

Malbork Castle by the River Nogat is one of the biggest castles in Europe.

My favourite day trip was to the enormous Wroclaw zoo!

17

Nature trails

Lots of people visit Poland for its amazing nature. There are forests, mountains, lakes, fields and even sand dunes to explore.

You can climb the towering sand dunes in Słowiński National Park.

Lurking in Poland's forests are bears, wolves, **wild boar**, wild cats and **elk**. In Masuria, 'the land of the lakes', look out for long-legged storks.

These rare, woolly European bison live in Białowieska National Park.

We camped by a lake. I got loads of mosquito bites – they were really itchy!

Outdoor explorer kit

- mosquito repellant
- binoculars
- comfy outdoor shoes

Time to eat

You will never feel hungry in Poland – the food is very filling! Polish people eat a lot of meat, including hundreds of types of sausage.

You'll be spoiled for choice in a Polish butchers!

Cabbage, beetroot and mushrooms are popular vegetables. For pudding, try a local cheesecake, gingerbread or doughnut.

Bigos (left) and pierogi (right) are traditional Polish foods.

On the menu

bigos (**be-**goss) - **stew with spiced meat and cabbage**

barszcz (**bah-**shch) - **beetroot soup**

pierogi (pee-er-**og**-ee) - **dumplings stuffed with meat, cheese and potatoes, or other fillings**

Going shopping

Market stalls are often set up in town squares, like this one in Cracow.

You'll come across many markets in Poland. These are where most people do their shopping. The money they spend is called the zloty.

Handcrafted amber jewellery and dice make great presents.

Why not buy a **souvenir** to take home? Look for Polish honey, paper crafts, woven mats, sheepskin slippers and amber jewellery.

Speak Polish!

amber, a shiny orange gem found on many Polish beaches
jantar (**yan**-tar)

traditional paper decoration
wycinanki (vee-chee-**non**-key)
(see pages 30-31)

Friendly faces

You will get a warm welcome from the Polish people – they love visitors! They are also very proud of their country.

This is a statue of Fredric Chopin, a famous Polish **composer** who died in 1849.

I saw Chopin's house – it had a massive piano!

Most Poles today are **Roman Catholic**. These girls are making their first Holy Communion.

No one forgets the millions of Polish people who were killed in the **Second World War**. Many of them were **Jews**. You will see lots of **memorials** in their honour.

Speak Polish!

hello/welcome
witam (vee-**tam**)

goodbye
do widzenia (do-veed-**zen**-ya)

yes
tak (tak)

no
nie (nee-**yeh**)

25

Having fun

The sports you find in Poland will depend on the season. Warm weather is good for watersports and fishing, while in winter some people head to the mountains to ski.

Poland has some fantastic scenery for walking holidays.

Football is popular at any time of year! The Polish people also like to dance.

People wear traditional costumes to perform Polish **folk dances**.

Activities to try

Mountains and forests – climbing, skiing, horseriding, biking

Lakes and sea – fishing, windsurfing, sailing, swimming

Time to celebrate!

If you visit Poland at Christmas or Easter, you'll probably run into a party! These are important religious celebrations, as well as times to have fun.

On Easter Monday, it is traditional to have a water fight.

I got soaked on Easter Monday – I had to go back to the hotel and change my clothes!

Christmas Eve is a big event. Families have a traditional meal and give each other presents before going to church to pray.

In Cracow, there is a competition to see who can make the best Christmas crib.

Festivals to catch

Fat Thursday (before Lent) feast on doughnuts filled with rose-petal jam!	Midsummer's Eve (21 June) float flowers and candles on a river or lake		

Make it yourself

Wycinanki are paper designs that Polish people often use to decorate their houses. Follow these steps to make your own wycinanki.

You will need:

- A3 sheet of plain, white paper
- pencil
- scissors
- colouring pencils or felt tips.

1. Fold the paper in half.

2. Copy the template (right) to draw a pattern against the fold – or design your own! What about a bunch of flowers or an animal?

3. Cut out the pattern through the double layer of paper. Don't cut along the fold. Be careful with the scissors!

4. Open out your wycinanki.

5. Colour it in and hang it in your window!

TIP: You could make several different wycinanki and glue them on top of each other in layers.

This room is painted with traditional Polish designs - they might give you ideas for your wycinanki.

Useful words

canal	A human-made river.
composer	Someone who writes music.
elk	A large type of deer.
folk dance	A traditional country dance.
Jew	A member of the Jewish religion. Jews worship in synagogues.
memorial	A statue or other special reminder of something that happened in the past.
Roman Catholic	A type of Christian. Roman Catholics worship in churches and cathedrals.
Second World War	A huge war that raged around the world from 1939 to 1945. It began when Germany invaded Poland.
souvenir	Something you take home to remind you of somewhere you have been.
spa town	A place where natural water from the ground is used for special treatments.
tram	A bus-like vehicle that runs on rails and is powered by electricity.
wild boar	A wild type of pig with greyish-brown skin.